Let's Read Aloud

On My Horse

By Eloise Greenfield • Illustrations by Jan Spivey Gilchrist

HarperFestival®

A Division of HarperCollins*Publishers*

I know it's not my horse,
the horse belongs to Mr. Morse
who owns the horse park where I go
every other week or so.

He helps me mount the horse and ride,
he's going to stay right by my side,
he's going to catch me if I fall
because the horse is very tall.

Bumpity down the path we go,
bumpity-bump, it's much too slow.
I wish that I could ride alone,
my horse and I out on our own.
  So . . .

I pretend
that riding on my horse,
I wave a high good-bye
to Mr. Morse
and disappear around the bend.
  And then

My horse and I are free,
we see a wide, wide
grassy space.
We race. Run past
a speeding rabbit.
My horse pumps his legs
fast,
pushes his neck
forward and back,
forward and back.
It makes me bounce.
I laugh loud.
On my horse
I laugh.

Now my horse walks
in the woods,
stepping through
          wildflowers,
stepping around a bush,
around a tree.
A leaf brushes my face,
softly.

We see a stream.
My horse wants to jump.
Not yet, I say,
let's trot a little way.
He trots to the music
I hear in my head,
I am riding, I am riding.
We come to a place
where the stream is wide.
Okay, I say, now *jump*!
 And he

JUMPS across
the stream in slow
magic motion.
We sail over the water,
slow.
We land lightly, no sound.
No sound.
I look around me, and I see
that we are back
where we began.
  Then . . .

Pretending is over and we are three,
Mr. Morse, my horse, and me.
It's time for us to say good-bye,
it's time to go, but I don't cry.
I think of when I'll come again
and all the things that we'll do then.
We'll visit mountains, rivers, sky,
we'll jump and run and swim and fly.
Just my horse and I.